A Race Against Time

Montana Paul

CONTENTS

ACKNOWLEDGMENTS

I want to thank the following people: Mrs. Emerick, Mrs. Zook, Mr. Pudewa, Mrs. Kessler, my mom for being my editor, my dad for giving me amazing ideas, and my sister, Makaylyn, for adding helpful insights. I love all you guys! Thank you for all you do.

CHAPTER ONE
A BROKEN TREATY

I remember it well. A day that changed my life for the better. This is how it started. I got up with my brother, Orlando. We quickly slipped our kilts on and ran out the door. Suddenly I remembered my pack, so I ran back inside to get it. It contained important stuff like: my money, slingshot, and a small dagger. I hurried to rejoin my brother. Then we bought breakfast from a beautiful young maiden. I've would've stopped to talk to her, but Orlando hurried me along. After breakfast, as usual, we got into mischief. Today, we would outwit Captain Draken, again.

My name is Antonio. I am a prince in The Mountain Kingdom in Elias, Scotland. I am originally from Spain. So how does a Spanish native become a Scottish prince? Well, I will briefly explain. I had a hard past, you see. My brother, Orlando, my family, and I were attacked by Vikings. My brother and I were the only ones to survive that ambush. All of my family had died.

We traveled to Scotland on horseback. We were very tired when we got here and looked for food. We stole a lot of food from a lot of people. We became excellent thieves, and even more skilled at not being caught by Draken, Captain of the King's guard. Thankfully, we discovered an abandoned cottage several miles outside of the village, and in the attic, we found a treasure chest! It also had kilts, hats, shoes, tights, and weapons. We lived on our own for quite a while, but one day, we got caught. We were brought before the king by Captain Draken. Expecting to be thrown into prison, the king surprised us by adopting us.

Here at The Mountain Kingdom there are millions of homes all lined up in a row. Water runs through the Eskdale River below the great La Amathistia Mountains. Flowers stand majestically in the grass. The village below my new home appears to be very tiny when I stand on the balcony of the palace. The little brick buildings remind me of my village in

Spain, and I think back to my childhood home. Our old house was very small, with a wooden deck and a small boat tied near it. But now I live in a castle, which is about 3 stories tall! It is made out of stone bricks stacked on top of each other. When you walk in, the big, lighted chandeliers amaze you as you walk on the huge, marble floor. The smell of peppermint fills the air throughout the entire castle since the cooks use it. There are about 16 bedrooms. When you walk in the throne room, however, some things change. It is lit by torches, and the flames glimmer on the marble floor. The two gold thrones are surrounded by guards. There is a big round table and one window. There is no opening from the roof into any part of the castle, and that's one way we keep bad guys away.

Across the mountains, there is another kingdom: The kingdom of Trevendell. We have a trading treaty with them. It states that they will buy wool only from us. Our kingdom has the finest wool taken from thousands of sheep, you see. We raise the sheep and shave their wool off and sell it to Trevendell, and they spin it and sell it to other countries. It's a win-win relationship, and our survival depends on it.

But sadly, two days ago the sheep got a

disease and a lot of the sheep died. Now, we don't have very much wool and the other kingdom has broken our treaty. Even the bravest knights are afraid to tell our father, King Alexander Kelsenack, the unfortunate news. So, it's up to me and Orlando to tell him. This is a heavy burden, though, since we love him and our kingdom.

"What?" Father shouted. "Trevendell has broken the treaty with us?"

I was quiet. So was Orlando. We had never seen our father so angry before. Our mother, Queen Abigail, put her hand on Father's wrist. When Father was a teenager, his parents had died in battle, but Father had a lot of leadership training and experience. He was good friends with the king of Trevendell, but he was furious when he heard that they had broken the treaty. Then he asked Captain Draken to take us out of the room. Draken was our guardian whenever the king asked him to be. I'm not sure he liked that task, given the history of mischief we caused him. But we had turned over a new leaf. A fresh start in life, and whatever he said was the law. He told us to stay by the door, but we heard Father and Mother talking.

"Alexander, can you calm down?" she asked.

"I'm worried about the kingdom," he said. "We need to save our people. Hotels are gone, businesses are closed down, and the treaty with Trevendell is broken," he continued. Mother took a deep breath. "Maybe we could look for a cure to the sickness in the Royal Library."

"Antonio! Orlando!" She called out. We came to them in an instant. "Please go to the Royal Library and research cures to sheep sickness." "Yes, Mother," and we hurried off.

****

We hunted all afternoon. We only found cures that we didn't need to sicknesses we no longer had, like that really bad whooping cough two years ago. I couldn't believe that just a year ago, we had hotels and restaurants and people bustling in to see all our wool products. They always said how glorious Scotland is. Scotland is generally cold, which makes the sheep grow the thickest, most luscious wool known in our part of the world. When we sheer our sheep in the spring, we fill all our warehouses and factories with enough wool to support the kingdom for an entire year. But now we can't, because of the sickness called "The Sheep Rash."

Orlando informed Father that we didn't find anything useful.

"That's okay. We can look again tomorrow," he said. We had a little free time left and didn't know how to spend it, so we went to our room. I stared out the window. Orlando grabbed a book and began to read. I quickly got bored of gazing out the window, so I decided to read also. I picked up a book and sat on my bed. The cool breeze blew through the window, and it flipped my pages. I turned the pages back. A few minutes later, I heard Orlando snoring, and I giggled to myself. I decided to sneak out and take my horse Tiberius for a secret ride, and also meet with my best friend, Gerald Copland.

****

"Antonio! Wait up!" Gerald tried to catch up with me. His horse, Thunder, ran as fast as he could, but to Thunder's surprise, Tiberius was faster. Together we raced down the hill. I crossed the finish line with Gerald close behind.

"Who's Gerald?" you might be wondering.

Well, he is the son of a high knight, Sir John Copland. Gerald used to sneak us food when we first arrived here, and he has been my best friend ever since. He gave me Tiberius when he was a young colt, and I have trained him these past few years. Gerald and I talked for what must have been an hour about life and about the worrisome sheep rash. Suddenly, I remembered something that made me say a hasty goodbye and I rode back quickly to the palace.

Orlando was waiting for me with a stern look on his face. We brothers were supposed to stay together when we went outside the castle. *"Oh, snap!"* I thought. *"Caught again."*

"Antonio!" Orlando scolded. "Remember when Captain Draken said that we had to be together when we go out of the castle gates?"

I gulped. I was in deep trouble with my brother, *and* Captain Draken. Unexpectedly, the Captain suddenly popped from around the corner.

"Antonio!" Captain Draken stared at me. I looked down at my feet.

"Yes?" I squeaked. I felt like a mouse.

To my surprise, Captain Draken blamed Orlando for taking a nap and not watching me. I felt awful.

"For your punishment," he said, "both of

you will sleep in the attic tonight." "Now go!"

We slowly climbed the creaky stairs to the attic. Trying to find a comfortable spot to sleep up there was nearly impossible. But eventually, we were sound asleep. As I drifted off I thought, *"I don't want to get in trouble tomorrow."*

CHAPTER 2
TRAINING FOR AN ADVENTURE

Orlando pulled back the curtains in the palace attic. I yawned. The attic was full of hay all the time, so I woke up with hay in my hair. Orlando laughed at me. I looked at him, and I sighed. Ready to begin researching in the library again, I begrudgingly got up and went downstairs. Orlando followed me after he finally stopped laughing. Draken was unusually happy and greeted us as if he had forgotten about yesterday. He excitedly pulled out a book and laid it on the table.

"This is what we have been looking for!"

"What?" I asked. Orlando and I were very curious.

"Something that can save the kingdom," he answered.

"What? You have something to save the kingdom?" We were both excided now.

"Yes. A red crystal," he answered.

We both stared at Draken. Draken had our undivided attention.

"Where?" asked Orlando.

"It is located in the La Amathistia Mountains, a three days journey," he replied.

"When can we begin the journey?" I inquired.

"It is a dangerous quest, so we must first prepare. You need to practice your sword fighting skills. We will leave in two days."

****

After breakfast, we grabbed our swords, and went to the training room. Draken was already waiting for us. He immediately took our swords away from us. *"Why did he do that?"* I thought. I looked at Orlando and guessed that he was thinking the same thing. Draken then took a few steps back.

"Now," he said. "You are going to try to get your swords back, using only your bodies."

I lunged at the arm holding my sword and punched it with my fists. The sword dropped and I quickly picked it up. Orlando tried to do the same thing but, it didn't work at all. Draken made it harder for him. Although Orlando was the oldest, he wasn't as fast as I was. Draken and Orlando fought over the sword for a very long time. Finally, Orlando managed to get the sword out of Draken's mighty hand. Orlando fell backward and quickly picked up his sword.

"Very good. Very good indeed." Draken said. "Next we are going to review basic fighting techniques. Orlando! Hand me your sword. Antonio and I will fight together first."

Orlando threw Draken the sword. I took a deep breath. Draken and I lunged at each other with our swords. He attacked from above, so I swung my blade upwards and his sword clashed with mine. I thought about each swing, and I aimed to get the other weapon from Draken. My plan worked, and I ended up with both blades. Draken started attacking with his muscular, sturdy hands. They were more powerful than I had imaged. I fell and dropped one of my swords. Draken tried to take it, but I swept it beyond his reach with my foot. Draken looked tired. I think I wore him out.

Breathless, he said, "The knowledge of the sword is strong in you, Antonio."

"I do not know what you mean, Captain," I

said.

"You have great skill, Antonio. You may grow up to be one of the great swordsmen of Scotland."

Orlando was not smiling. He didn't like to hear that his younger brother was better than he was. He brushed his kilt, stretched his legs, and prepared to fight. Up went his sword. He was ready to show off his great skill. They lunged at each other. This time, Draken attacked from below, almost making a tear in Orlando's kilt. He protected it with his blade. Their swords clashed and the sound of iron striking iron filled the air. Orlando cut Draken's arm. Draken cut Orlando's neck. I gulped. Even with their wounds, they kept fighting. Gritting his teeth, Orlando never gave up.

Orlando won, slightly wounded, but triumphant. We went to our room to rest. He hurt all over, and I felt sorry for him. I thought it was odd that Draken didn't say a word after his defeat. He looked worried, and I was confused. Draken didn't even say he was sorry for hurting Orlando, but I put it out of my mind. Mother came to tend to his wounds, and Father pulled me aside.

"I want you to go on the journey with

Draken, the loyal knights, and Orlando."

"I want to help the kingdom," I hesitated. "I'm good, but not as good as a knight."

"Draken said you fought well today. He was impressed."

"But Father, I don't want to go on the journey."

"Antonio, I want you to go. I trust in you."

"Father, I fear that I will not survive."

"Antonio, I believe in you."

****

I couldn't sleep that night. I worried that Orlando wouldn't get better, that I would die if I went on the journey, and I had an unsettling feeling about Captain Draken. I didn't know how to explain it, or where it came from. I didn't want to be so anxious. Orlando was lying down in his bed, but I sat up in mine: thinking. I looked at Orlando. I looked around the room. I had to get some rest. I finally lied down and closed my eyes. It took a while, but I eventually fell asleep.

CHAPTER 3
LOVE AT FIRST SIGHT

Orlando healed quickly and was fine the next day. Our Mother's special salve and bandages always healed wounds quickly. Captain Draken taught us more skills that day. Later, we both went to the village with Draken because we needed to retrieve all the supplies we needed for our three-day journey. When we were looking in a store window, I bumped into a pretty young maiden.

"Pardon me," I said.

"Pardon me," she answered. I was awestruck by her radiant beauty. I could barely speak.

"Wha-what is your name?" I stuttered.

"Ella. What is yours?" Her voice was as soothing as an angel's voice.

"Antonio," I replied. I couldn't stop gazing at her.

"Good day," Ella said.

"Goo-good day," I stammered, and she walked away.

I couldn't believe that I had just met and talked with an angel! Orlando caught up with me. He saw me smiling.

"Why are you smiling?" he asked.

"I met a girl. Her name is Ella."

"Ohh," Orlando retorted. "You met a girl?"

"Yes," I replied, staring off in the distance. "A girl, but not just any girl, she was the most beautiful creature I have ever seen in my entire life!"

"Better catch up with Draken," Orlando interrupted, smacking me on the shoulder. "He will be wondering where we are."

We ran through the village to find our Captain. We looked and looked. Neither of us could find him. We searched some more, and ran into Gerald.

"What brings you here, Your Majesties?" he said. "May I point you in the right direction?"

"I am looking for Captain Draken," I replied, beginning to worry where he was.

"Aye, he told me that he had to visit Sir

Benjamin Kent," Gerald said with a smile. "He told me to be on the lookout for two young teenage princes in green kilts with swords at their sides and to tell them where he was. So, here you are, and there he is at the third cottage on the right- at Forbes Brew."

"Oh, and by the way, you still owe me a fair horse race." Gerald declared, as he turned to leave.

"Perhaps when we get back from our journey," I countered. *If we even survive it,* " I thought.

"Aye. Have a good one!" he said, and ran down the road.

****

We entered the pub. We were greeted by the smells, sounds, and bustle of a typical Scottish tavern, and…there was Ella!

"Well, Antonio," she said. "Nice to see your face again so soon. May I help you in any way?"

I loved her sweet voice. "Yes. We looking for Captain Draken and a Sir Benjamin Kent," I replied.

"I have not seen them," she answered.

"May we look?"

"Certainly," she replied. "Is there anything

else, Your Majesties?"

"No," I stated. But secretly, there was so much more I wanted to ask her as she slipped away.

"Did you tell her that we were royal?" Orlando whispered.

"I did not," I wondered aloud.

We followed Ella to the back room, and suddenly she stopped, totally stunned. Immediately somebody stood up to greet us. It was Draken's friend, Sir John Copland.

"Well there, I see that my son, has obeyed and led you little foxes right into Draken's trap."

"What?" I exclaimed.

"How dare you speak to the princes of Scotland like that?" Orlando yelled.

"Gerald?" I muttered to myself, "He betrayed me?"

"Yes!" Copland said, with a laugh.

"He couldn't!" I thought. "I don't believe it!" I said definitively. Suddenly, Gerald appeared through the back door. He pulled out his sword. I unsheathed mine. Instead of attacking me, he grabbed Ella and started out the back door. My best friend had betrayed me!

"How could you do that, Gerald?" I yelled.

"You couldn't understand. It's too

complicated."

"But...." I was cut short by a slam, as Gerald and Ella disappeared out the back door. Without a thought, I burst into the alley, just in time to see Gerald swinging Ella onto Thunder, and galloping down the alley. "Help!" screamed Ella.

"I'm coming Ella!" I hollard back, and I leapt onto Tiberius and dashed down the alley after them at top speed.

CHAPTER 4
THE EVIL TRUTH

By the time I caught up with Gerald, he had Ella tied up, and looking like a poor victim.

"It is your choice, Prince Antonio. Fight me and get your beautiful Ella back, or retreat and loose Ella forever."

"Don't retreat! Please!" Ella screamed.

"I will fight you, for Ella and for my kingdom!" I exclaimed.

I swung my sword at him, and he dropped Ella. I tried to catch her, but she slipped from my grasp. One of the king's guards quickly came to her aid. Gerald and I kept fighting. Tiberius cut in front of Thunder, and Gerald fell as his horse stumbled. I could see that Ella was free, so I turned Tiberius to face Gerald. He stood, sword in hand, and I galloped toward him. As I swung at him, he sliced my hand, and I dropped the reins. It was bleeding all over. We kept swinging our blades at each other, and I swung my blade across his face.

"Ahh!" he yelled in pain.

"You deserved that!" I sneered.

He swung his sword and sliced my leg. I fell from Tiberius and hit my head on the hard gravel, which knocked me unconscious.

****

I awoke and looked all around me, but everything was blurry. I couldn't tell where I was. Immediately my head reminded me of the battle. I moaned.

"Ella?"

"I'm here," she replied. I smiled at her sweet voice.

"Where's Orlando? Where am I? And how did I get here?"

"Orlando is here, and you're in your bed in the palace. The king's guards came to our rescue and carried you to safety. Unfortunately, Gerald got away."

When I could finally focus, Ella's beauty filled my gaze. I loved her right then and there. I never wanted to be away from her again. I feasted my eyes upon her, and her smile captivated me. But I knew duty to my kingdom was calling.

"I'm glad you're okay. I was worried about you," she said. She took my hand.

"Your hands are cold."

"Don't worry about me," I replied. "Ella, I must tell you something. I am going to get the crystal with Sir Benjamin and Orlando before Draken does."

Sir Benjamin was not a friend of Draken, but a loyal Knight to The Mountain Kingdom.

He was to someday take Draken's place as Captain after he retired. Today was the day he unexpectedly received that promotion! Sir Kent was strong, loyal, and well respected by all the knights and the King, himself.

"You can't go," Ella said.

"Why?" I asked.

"You can't leave me!"

"I wish I could stay, too. But when I get better, I am going on the journey."

I assured Ella that I would be safe and careful. All of a sudden I was no longer afraid of the journey, but longed to prove my courage. Once again, Mother's salve worked its wonders, and I was healed overnight. That meant that in the morning, it was time for an adventure. I couldn't wait until all this was over.

CHAPTER 5
A JOURNEY BEGINS
WITH ITS FIRST STEP

I woke up feeling wonderful, but soon I was flooded with old worries again. It was the day I would start a very dangerous journey to save the kingdom. What if Draken was lying about the crystal? What if it was located in another place besides the La Amathistia Mountains? What if there was no crystal at all? Then the kingdom will be devastated. I was worried about Ella, too. I didn't want to leave her in a tumultuous kingdom all alone.

After getting dressed, I tiptoed down the steps to get something to eat. Ella was down there. So were Orlando and Sir Benjamin.

"Hello, my lady," I said as I kissed her hand.

Ella blushed. "Well, good morning, Antonio."

"I see that you woke up earlier than I did, Orlando," I said.

"Indeed I did," Orlando replied. "But then again, I'm not the one who got myself hurt this time," he laughed.

"Are you ready, men?" Sir Benjamin asked. "We are going to leave soon."

"We are ready," we both declared.

"Well then, I will get the horses ready," Sir Benjamin stood and excused himself and Orlando followed.

As their footsteps faded, I talked with Ella.

"Promise me that you will come back," she said.

"I can't promise that, Ella."

"Then take me with you," Ella pled. "I am a good fighter."

"The journey is too dangerous for you," I replied. "I wish I could stay, but I have to go."

"Please take me."

"I can't." I finally had to say, "I love you."

She started to hug me, and I kissed her hand again.

"I must go."

"Please take me," Ella begged. "I would rather go than stay in this depressing kingdom."

"Fine, but you must stay close to me," I relented. Ella hugged me again. I was somewhat relieved that I had decided she could come, but that meant extra challenges, for there was going to be a lady accompanying us on our expedition.

Within an hour, we mounted our horses and began the journey. Ella rode with me, and Orlando was close behind. We came upon the main road leading to the mountains, but Sir Benjamin led us on a path I didn't expect. Was he going to betray us like Draken did?

"Why are we taking this way?" I asked.

"Your father says it is a shorter and faster way," Benjamin answered.

"Oh," Orlando interjected.

"Whew! That could have been worse!" I thought.

We came upon a secret, dark cave that Sir Benjamin said would lead us through the mountain. "We can take a short-cut through this cave, since our enemies got a one day head start," Sir Kent reasoned. "And that puts us closer to the crystal."

We ignited torches and led the horses into the cave. Suddenly, I heard growling. Where was it coming from? I aimed my torch toward the sound and met a wolf.

The wolf let out a hideous growl. I swung out my sword. It ran at me. Then a pack of wolves started attacking us.

"Run!" I told Ella.

I swung my sword at the wolf. It jumped on top of me, but I pushed it off. Two wolves were attacking Orlando. They jumped on top of him and his torch went dark.

"ORLANDO!"

CHAPTER 6
RECOVERY

I listened for a reply from Orlando, but none came. Another wolf snapped at me. I swung my sharp blade through his back. After the rest of the wolf pack fled, Ella came back.

"Ella, what are you doing here!" I shouted.

"I need to get Orlando to safety. He's injured."

Dragging Orlando out of the cave, she left. Sir Benjamin grabbed a torch, and we all made it out of the cave.

****

We made camp that night on the other side of the mountain. Father's shortcut had saved us time, but rattled our nerves. We talked into the night about what we might encounter the next day, and we let Orlando rest from the wolf attack against a tree. Luckily, I had some of Mother's magical salve with me, and I put it on Orlando's wounds. When I was sitting near the fire warming my freezing hands, Ella walked up to me.

"Sorry about that," she said.

"Sorry about what?" I asked.

"For coming back and putting myself in danger."

"It's okay, Ella," I answered.

"Can you convince me that you really forgive me?"

"Of course, Ella." I passionately kissed her hand.

I turned to Sir Benjamin. "What is the plan?" I asked.

"We first go west toward the La Amathistia Mountains," he began. "If Draken, Sir Copland, and Gerald are in our way, we fight."

"That's it?" I asked.

"I think so," he replied.

"I think we should go north," Orlando added, limping toward us.

"*You*, Orlando, should go rest," Ella said.

"It's okay, Ella," he replied as she tried to help him over. "I can walk by myself."

Orlando limped to the tree stump and sat down.

Orlando and Sir Benjamin talked about the plan. Ella came to me.

"Antonio," she began, "I've been wanting to say something. Over the last several days, our relationship has grown. I wanted to tell you something that might give you more bravery. I love you."

She loves me! I thought. *Should I kiss her or not? We both love each other, so maybe I should. I will!* I grabbed her, stood up, caressed her face, and we shared our first kiss. I gazed longingly into her eyes. She was right. I did have more bravery than ever before.

And at the same moment, we both said, "I love you."

****

The next day, I woke up early to the cool morning air. Orlando's wounds were healed. When I looked at them, I thought, "*Man, Mother's salve does work wonders. Maybe I should learn how to make it.*"

We journeyed on. Orlando rode ahead of Sir Benjamin. I rode behind him, keeping careful watch for any danger, ready to pull out my sword and fight Draken and his crew. Ella sat behind me on Tiberius, having her hands placed around my waist. But no one knew that our lives would be changed forever in the next few moments. It all began when Orlando shouted,

"I have found the crystal, but it's in Gerald's hands!"

CHAPTER 7
NOT ALL IS WHAT IT SEEMS

I jumped off Tiberius and ran as fast as I could with my weapon at my side. I knew Gerald was working with Draken now, so he was an enemy, but I was having a hard time coming to terms with his betrayal.

I met him face to face and drew my sword. I stayed in front of Ella because I couldn't let her be hurt in any way. Orlando and Sir Benjamin drew their blades too, and we were surrounded by Gerald, Draken, and several of their traitorous friends.

Draken grabbed the crystal and ran away with it, and his comrades followed. Sir Benjamin and Orlando gave chase toward the mountains. My eyes were locked on Gerald.

We were fighting in between the mountains and the edge of the lush forest. I fought him, protecting Ella at the same time. Gerald swung his sword at my neck, and I ducked trying to not get the dreadful strike. I tried to attack him, but it was difficult. We had practiced our fencing many times together over the years and knew each other's weaknesses.

I tried to get Ella to run to safety, but she refused and ran toward Tiberius, unsheathing an extra sword from his pouch. She then charged toward Captain Draken's men. *"Fine,"* I thought. *"Let her fight. She's good with a sword,"* I encouraged myself, but I didn't want to lose her.

Gerald attacked my side, and I dodged just in time. I tried to strike him again, but I missed.

Iron angrily struck iron. After about fifteen minutes, I could barely hold my sword. I could tell Gerald was exhausted too, because he was panting like a dog. After a couple minutes more, I finally managed to swing my sword and slice his arm, and before he could say anything, I stabbed him.

"Why?" he moaned.

"Why? Why did *you* betray *me*? Why did *you* leave *me* after all these years?"

"I-I-" He tried to speak.

Gerald fell to the ground. He died with his

eyes open. I pulled my sword out of him. Wiping it on the ground, I glanced back at him. "Goodbye, my old friend Gerald," I said sorrowfully. "Sorry that I had to kill you, but it's called "Justice." And I had to win today."

After I collected my thoughts, I ran toward the mountain to see who to fight next.

CHAPTER 8
THE CRYSTAL'S DESTINY

"Well, if it isn't the worthless young prince of Scotland I have encountered!"

I spun around, and Draken let out an evil chuckle.

"It *was* you and all of your men who went and got the crystal before we did," I concluded. "You have been secretly plotting all this time?"

"Yes," Draken declared. "It was me."

I drew my sword out and pointed it at him.

"Your choice is to either fight and die, or surrender and live the rest of your life in a cold, cramped, smelly, and damp prison cell. I'd call you 'Captain' but I'm sure you've figured out by now you've been replaced."

Draken huffed, squared his shoulders, and drew his sword. It was decided. We were going to fight.

We circled each other for what seemed an eternity. Then blades met in the air. I held my blade tightly, but I lost it. Draken picked it up. With my fists, I knocked my blade out of his hands, and we continued the dramatic fight.

Clang! Swoosh! Scrape! My blade worked the movements. I held my own, waiting, dodging, planning, and waiting some more for my opportunity. Then, I jumped up into the air, flipped over Draken's head, and landed on my feet behind him, simultaneously stabbing Draken in the back with my sword. I spun around to see Draken fall down the side of the mountain.

"Draken!" Sir John Copland cried. He was fighting with Orlando. He let out an evil smile and stabbed Orlando in the heart.

"NO!!!!!!" I screamed, and so did Ella.

This can't be! I thought.

"Arggh!" I ran down the mountain toward Copland. He charged at me sword-in-hand, but I dodged his blow and sliced him. Sir John Copland dropped to the ground and the other knights fled from the carnage.

"Orlando!" Ella screamed, running toward him. She held the crystal in her hands. Orlando opened his eyes.

"Ella," he began. "Goodbye. Take good

care of my brother."

He turned to me. "Antonio," he coughed, "Thank you. You were always the better brother."

To his faithful man he said, "Sir Kent, thank you for your loyalty. We saved the kingdom."

He slowly closed his eyes, and was gone.

I put him on my horse and carried him home.

****

During the mournful trek back home we hardly spoke a word. We also wondered how much worse the kingdom had gotten.

After riding through the palace gates and dismounting, we searched for the king and handed him the crystal. We followed him to the throne room. He held the crystal high above his head and something mysterious happened.

CHAPTER 9
THE BEAUTIFUL QUESTION

The throne room window was open and a sunbeam struck the crystal. It shined so bright that we were nearly blinded. A red spark sprang from the crystal like a lightning bolt and blasted toward the mountain. Suddenly, a gigantic cave formed where there once stood rocks and trees. Something was glittering inside the mountain cave. Ella jumped up and down with excitement. Benjamin laughed soulfully. I smiled, but I grieved for my brother.

Father ordered Benjamin to organize miners and to head back to the mountain.

When they left, Father asked me, "Where is Orlando?"

"He did not survive the journey." I turned

away from my father's gaze. "He's on my horse."

We returned to where Tiberius was standing. Orlando lay across his saddle. Father picked him up gently. A tear came down his face. Suddenly, Orlando opened his eyes. He looked straight at Father.

"Father?" Orlando whispered. Turning his head, he spoke again, "Antonio?"

"Orlando?" Father and I exclaimed at the same time, totally astounded.

Father let Orlando down slowly. To our amazement, he could stand! He ran straight towards me. Then, for the first time in a long time, we embraced.

"You're alive!" I exclaimed.

Orlando nodded.

I couldn't believe it. He *was* alive!

"The crystal must have healed you!" I said inquisitively.

"I think it did!" Orlando proclaimed.

Father hugged both of us at the same time. We had never felt happier.

****

Early the next week, Sir Benjamin came back to us with gold in his hands.

"Look at it!" Benjamin said. I could tell he was happy. I was happy, too. In fact, I think *everyone* was happy.

"Well," I said, "that *is* a lot of gold."

Sir Kent laughed, "You wouldn't believe how much more there is! The kingdom will be wealthy for centuries."

While Sir Benjamin spoke with the king and Orlando, Ella and I slipped away and enjoyed the sunset by ourselves.

"Everything is perfect," Ella mused. "It's funny. When Orlando was magically healed, so were all the sheep. Now the treaty with Trevendell has been restored, and the Kingdom is saved. And I am here with you."

****

The next morning Ella and I walked along the rocky edge of the hillside below the castle. Suddenly, stones slid from under her feet, and Ella would have fallen if she did not reach for my hand. As quick as a flash, our hands clasped around each other's, and I lifted her up to safety. We fixed our eyes on each other, smiling. I pulled her close, brushing a lock of red hair out of her eyes.

"I told you 'you have to stay close to me,' " I teased.

"Well, I'll have to get better at that," Ella replied. "I don't want to give you a heart attack."

"Well, you almost did for a second."

Then it happened. The thought came to my mind, *Ask her. Now's the perfect time! You love her, Antonio, and you know it.*

As if on cue, I bent down on one knee.

Ella gasped. "Antonio?"

"My dearest Ella, will you become my wife?"

"Oh, Antonio…YES!"

I jumped to my feet. She hugged me. We both let out a tear of joy.

"Yes," she whispered in my ear.

I looked her fully in the face. "Oh, Ella."

She grabbed my hand and kissed it. Then, I cupped her cheeks gently in my hands and I kissed her.

We embraced once again, and she said, "Antonio, I love you with all my heart."

"I do too, Ella," I replied. "Let's go back and tell my parents."

"Okay." She replied.

We made our way back to the palace. Hand in hand, walking in the sunshine.

"Well, Antonio," Father said, "I see that you have returned. Mother and I were just talking about you two."

"Aye," I said. "And we have exciting news."

"What?" he asked.

"Ella and I are in fact," I looked at her before answering, "engaged."

"Well, that is exciting!" Father laughed.

"I'm so happy for you," Mother exclaimed and she gave Ella a long embrace.

That same evening, Mother, Father and I talked about the news in private.

"So, you've known Ella since the beginning of June." Father said.

"That is correct." I said.

"And you are *sure* you want to marry her?"

"Yes."

"And you want the wedding to be next February?"

"Yes."

"Well then, let's plan a royal wedding!" The Queen announced.

"Thank you."

We stood up and hugged. I felt like it was the best time of my life.

I ran out the door to where Ella was waiting.

"They said yes!"

CHAPTER 10
NEW BEGINNINGS, AGAIN

Nine months of tireless preparation rushed by like the blink of an eye, and the biggest day of my life had begun. I slipped on my finest kilt, and I smiled at the mirror. I was as nervous as a mouse running away from a very mean and fat cat. I took a deep breath. I stood up straight. I walked down the hallway like the proudest knight.

I entered the throne room where Ella and I would be married. The room was crowded. I stood at the front near my father, hands clasped behind my back. The doors slowly opened. All the people were standing now. The Scottish music started.

As Ella walked down the aisle, I couldn't

help but stare. Her face was radiant. Her auburn, flowing locks fell gracefully across her shoulders. I studied her gorgeous dress. Her hands were clasping her rose bouquet, which matched her hair perfectly. The lace on her dress was shaped like a beautiful butterfly flying over the green land. I smiled. Ella was like a bright, green package, waiting to be unwrapped on Christmas morning.

When she made it to the end of her majestic entrance, I took her hand and said, "Are you ready for this?"

"Ready for anything," she boasted.

We nervously wrapped our hands in each other's. As instructed, I put the ring around her finger and gave my promise. Then she took my hand and did the same. Then she said the two words I would forever love, "I do."

I had butterflies in my stomach when my father finally said, "Son, you may kiss your bride." With that, Ella and I kissed. The people, of course, cheering, were excited more than ever before.

****

The cool breeze blew through the window as I walked into the room. Ella walked up to me. I smiled at my new wife.

"You look tired, dear." Ella noticed the weary look on my face.

"I'm not tired," I replied, kissing Ella on the forehead.

"You look like it," Ella responded.

"I'm a little worn out," I began, "especially after all that wonderful cake Mother made and all that dancing."

"I see."

"I'm glad we're finally married."

"I am too."

"I love you very much, Ella."

"I love you, Antonio."

We collapsed on the couch, and whispered all night. We kept saying how wonderful our special day was: the cake, the dancing, and everything else.

"Wasn't our day perfect?" Ella asked.

"Yes," I answered. And it was.

ABOUT THE AUTHOR

Montana Paul lives in Central Indiana with her family, her stuffed animal buddies, and her pets. Writing is one of her passions. When not writing a novel or short story, she is usually playing her harp, studying science, reading, drawing, trying to fix something, or playing the Wii. Whatever she is doing, her main goal is to do everything to the glory of God.

Made in the USA
Monee, IL
18 August 2022